This book belongs to:

_____

_____

_____

First published 2011 by Walker Books Ltd
87 Vauxhall Walk, London SE11 5HJ

This edition published 2012

2 4 6 8 10 9 7 5 3 1

© 2011 Lucy Cousins
Lucy Cousins font © 2011 Lucy Cousins

The author/illustrator has asserted her moral rights
Illustrated in the style of Lucy Cousins by King Rollo Films Ltd
Maisy™. Maisy is a registered trademark of Walker Books Ltd, London

Printed in China

British Library Cataloguing in Publication Data:
a catalogue record for this book is
available from the British Library

ISBN 978-1-4063-4455-4

www.walker.co.uk

Maisy Goes to the City

Lucy Cousins

WALKER BOOKS
AND SUBSIDIARIES

LONDON · BOSTON · SYDNEY · AUCKLAND

Maisy and Charley have come to visit Dotty for the weekend.

Coach Station

"Welcome to the city!" Dotty calls. She's just moved here.

The road outside is really busy.
BROOM, VROOM, BEEP!

What a lot of traffic, and what giant buildings!

The streets are crowded,
so you have to walk quite slowly.

There are lots and
LOTS of shops.

"Come and see the toyshop," Dotty says. "It's huge!"

When the signal goes green, it's safe to cross.

The store is full of shoppers!
Charley likes the escalators.
Maisy likes the lifts.

The toys are fabulous!
Charley wants to buy
them all.

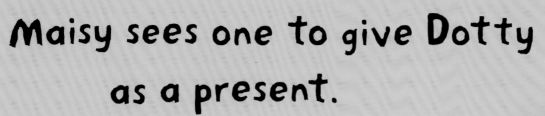

Maisy sees one to give Dotty
as a present.

She pays for it, but—
oh dear!
Where are
the others
now?

"Are you lost?"
Suddenly Maisy
wishes she was
safe at home.

Peacock makes an announcement on the intercom.

"There you are, Maisy!" Dotty holds her friend's hand tightly.

Time to eat!
Dotty brings them
to a café in a square.

A busker plays music, and the friends share a pizza.

Afterwards they play.
Even the park is busy in
the city!

To get to Dotty's flat, they need to take an underground train.

"Our stop's on the blue line," Dotty says.

It's a squash in the carriage.

Hang on tight, everyone!

"It's been a lovely day!" says Charley.
"Thank you for having us to stay,"
says Maisy.

It's nearly dark.
The stars are shining.

The city lights are bright
and busy too. They'll go
twinkle, twinkle, twinkle
all night long.

My friend Maisy

ISBN 978-1-4063-0970-6

ISBN 978-1-4063-0972-0

ISBN 978-1-4063-0971-3

ISBN 978-1-4063-0976-8

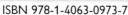

ISBN 978-1-4063-0973-7

ISBN 978-1-4063-0974-4

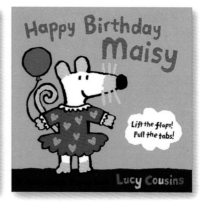

ISBN 978-1-4063-0691-0

It's more fun with Maisy!

Available from all good booksellers

www.maisyfun.com